Lucy lives at
64 Zoo Lane,
right next door
to the zoo. Every
night, she climbs
out of her window,
slides down the long
long neck of Georgina
the Giraffe and listens to
one of the animals
tell her a story . . .

...and tonight it's the

GEORGINA THE GIRAFFE
written and illustrated by An Vrombaut
Book based on 'The Story of Georgina the Giraffe' of the TV series
64 Zoo Lane written by An Vrombaut and John Grace.

© Millimages S.A. / Zoo Lane Productions Ltd 2001

British Library Cataloguing in Publication Data
A catalogue record of this book is available from the British Library.

ISBN-13: 978 0340 78861 5

The right of An Vrombaut to be identified as the author and illustrator
of this Work has been asserted by her in accordance with
the Copyright, Designs and Patents Act 1988.

First edition published 2001
1

Published by Hodder Children's Books
a division of Hachette Children's Books
338 Euston Road London NW1 3BH

Printed in China
All rights reserved

This edition published 2007
for Index Books Ltd

story of **Georgina** the Giraffe

An Vrombaut

Hodder Children's Books

A division of Hachette Children's Books

Georgina the Giraffe had many talents. She could sing and dance and do all sorts of tricks with her long neck. One day, Georgina had a brilliant idea. 'I want to invite all my friends to the Georgina Giraffe Show!' she said. And she did.

The next day all the animals
gathered at the Blue Mountain.
Everyone was very excited.
'Welcome, welcome,' said Georgina
and she sang her song.

'I am tall, very tall,

I am **taller** than you all! I can reach very **high**, to the clouds in the sky!

I am pretty, I am witty! I'm Georgina ballerina, Prima donna, concertina. I'm so clever, I'm the best. I'm much better than the rest!

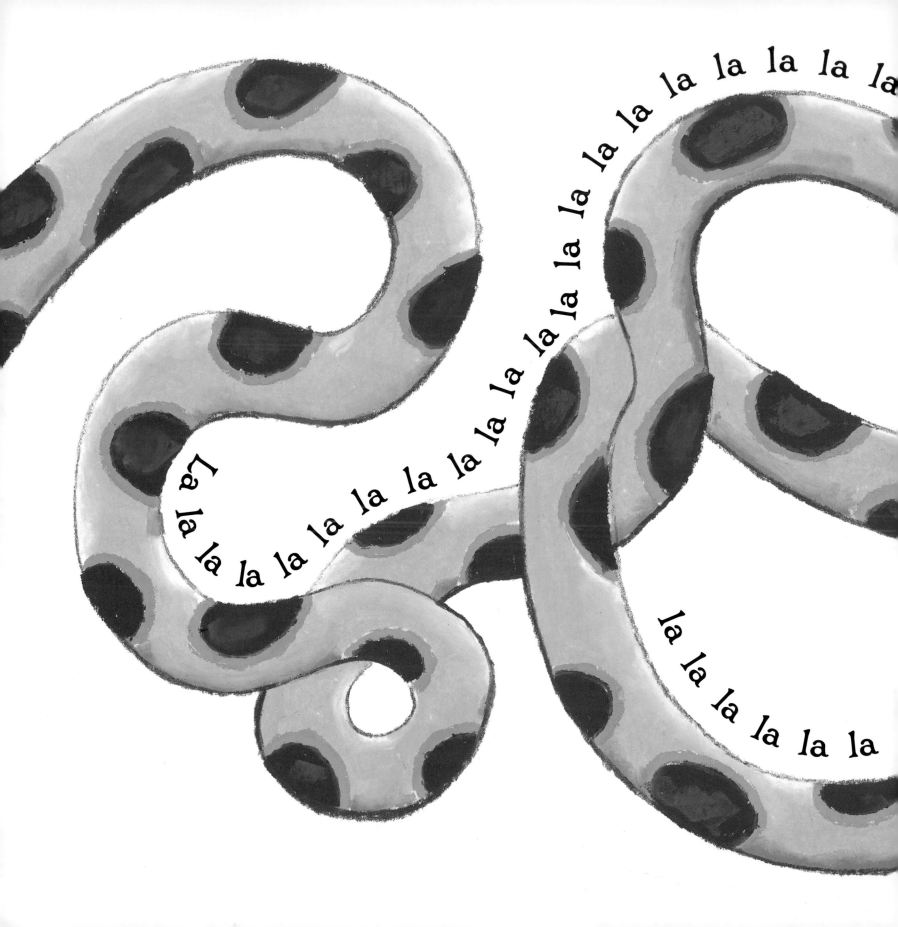

La la la la la la la la la la la la la la la la la la la la la la la la la la la

Ouch!'

Georgina the Giraffe finished
her song with a knot in her neck!
And, instead of applause, there was
only laughter from her friends.
'Serves you right for showing off
like that,' said Nelson the Elephant.
Georgina sobbed. 'I didn't mean
what I said about being better
than the rest.'

Molly the Hippo felt sorry for Georgina. 'Come on,' she said. 'Let's see if we can help.' The animals pulled and tugged at Georgina's neck, but it was no use. The knot was too tight.

Then Giggles had a clever idea. 'Why don't we take Georgina to our Uncle Gordon? He's a Knot Doctor and knows all about knots!'

So Giggles and Tickles took Georgina to their Uncle Gordon, who lived far, far away on the other side of the **Blue Mountain**.

When they arrived lots
of animals were waiting
to see Doctor Gordon.

There was a chameleon with a Tongue-Twister-Knot.

Two elephants with a Catch-The-Slippery-Fruit-Knot.

A lion with a Fly-Swatter-Knot.

A flamingo with a Pretty-Party-Knot.

And a snake with a Very-Knotty-Sort-Of-Knot.

Georgina waited for a long, long time. But finally a voice from the cave bellowed, 'NEXT!'

Inside
the cave
Doctor Gordon
Gorilla was reading
his knot book.
'Our friend Georgina
was singing La la la,'
Giggles and Tickles
explained, 'and now she's
got a knot.'
Doctor Gordon looked at
Georgina with a serious frown.
'It looks like you've got
a Big-Show-Off-Knot,' he muttered.

But then he smiled. 'Don't worry,
Georgina! To get better all you have
to do is sing La la la backwards!'
'But what is La la la
backwards?' asked Georgina.
Doctor Gordon looked in
his knot book. 'Ah,'
he said. 'Here it is. La la la
backwards is Al al al!'

So Georgina sang:

al al al al al

'Al al al al

al al al al al al al al

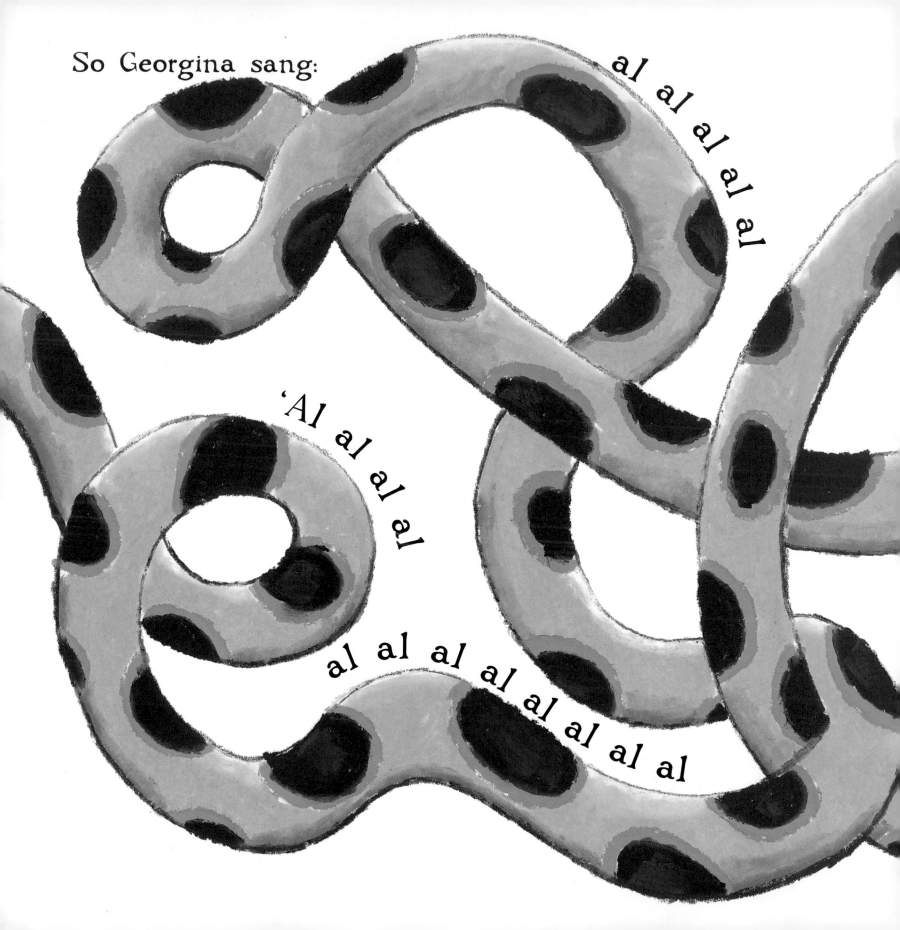

And the knot was gone.
'**Hooray!**' cheered Giggles and Tickles.

Georgina was better. And now she knew how lucky she was to have such **good friends!**